ACTUS IN EXSPE

The Magic House

The Amazing Adventures of Alexander and Sophia

By Alan Matkovic

With illustrations by Justo Borrero

ISBN 978-0692953785

www.themagichousestory.com

Toddler fun adventures

Acknowledgements

First and foremost, I would like to thank my three children. They have been an endless source of inspiration for me to create The Magic House and all the other nightly bedtime stories they have heard time and again. Without these adorable little souls, there would be no tales to tell. They are the light of my life, and I love nothing more than to spend time with them playing and creating.

A big thank you to my beautiful wife who birthed the kids, is a wonderful mother, and has always been supportive of my writing.

Special thanks to the erudite and brilliant Laurel Fishman for her editing prowess. Her mastery of the English language and adept eye for polishing are unrivaled.

And finally, many thanks to the great Justo Borrero for his lively and lovely, fantastic illustrations. He is a true artist who lives and breathes his craft. It was such a pleasure to work with him.

I love you all!

Alan Matkovic

September 2017

Once upon a time, there was a little boy named Alexander and a little girl named Sophia. They liked to play outside, especially on the beach. One day they were playing at the beach when they looked off into the distance to see a brightly colored house on top of a hill.

Its purple, orange and green colors seemed to shimmer in the sunlight. Bubbling with excitement, Sophia and Alexander looked at each other and said at the same time, "That must be a magic house! Let's explore it!"

The children swiftly gathered snacks for their intended journey, filling their backpack with raisins, applesauce, crackers, pretzels and water. Just in case, they brought their hats, jackets and boots, even some rope. You never know what you'll need on an adventure.

Alexander and Sophia first had to cross a large expanse of sand, but the thought of reaching the magic house made the long walk go by quickly. The adventurers soon met a field of very tall grass, which they easily slipped through like curtains flowing in the breeze. The grass ended, and large rocks and boulders lay ahead.

The kids brought out their rope and used it to climb up the huge obstacles. After passing through the sand, grass and boulders, Alexander and Sophia had to ascend a big hill. They put on their boots and trudged upward.

By the time Alexander and Sophia reached the top of the hill, they were tired and hungry. So they snacked on applesauce and thirstily gulped down cold water. As they looked around, there before them was the magic house! The twins ran up to it expecting to find a front door, but there was no door at all. Quickly they zipped around the outside of the house; however, they did not find a single door or window. *A magic house must have a magic entrance*, Alexander and Sophia thought.

They turned over rocks looking for a special key, and repeated magic words and phrases they knew: "Shazam!" "Open sesame!" "Alakazam!" "Abracadabra, o-pen-up!" But none of those magic words worked. Hmmmmm…

Alexander sat down against a big apple tree to mull over what to do. But just then, Sophia excitedly ran over to him, “Look, Alexander! Look at that branch above you. It’s the color of gold, a golden branch. That must be a secret switch!” Alexander immediately leaped up and pulled down on the golden branch. *Voilà*, a little door appeared on the magic house!

They scurried through the small opening not wider than a beach ball, and entered a hall lined with unusual doors numbered: 1, 2, 3, 4, 5, 6, 7. Like the outside of the house, the passageway was colorfully lit, with yellow stars on the ceiling, bright orange sides and a glowing purple floor. The door immediately to the left of them had a 1 on the outside.

They cautiously opened it up to see what appeared to be a pool — not of water, but of pink and purple jelly beans! Millions of them! Alexander and Sophia jumped in, swam in the jelly beans, ate a bunch, and stuffed many more in their pockets. When they were totally jelly-beaned out, Sophia said, "Let's see what's in the next room!"

The next door was aqua blue and had gleaming white crescent moons on it, with the number 2 in the middle. They carefully opened it up. Cold air blew against their curious faces.

Inside, Sophia and Alexander saw a large room filled with mounds of snow and a pond of ice in the middle! They noticed pink and purple ice skates next to the door, which perfectly fit their little feet. Eagerly they skated around and around the pond.

After twirling too fast on the ice, they spun into a snowbank. A pile of snow fell on their heads. And they giggled.

Covered in snow, they decided to build a snowman.

Then they created a snow house, where Alexander and Sophia snacked and played. When they started to get chilly, the kids decided to explore another room.

The next door was a lovely reddish amber color, labeled number 3. With a tingle of excitement, they opened up the door. Their eyes and ears were delighted by an array of instruments playing beautiful music. There were violins, cellos, pianos, drums, flutes and horns — even an accordion. The children sat and listened, entranced by the melodious sounds. Alexander and Sophia each picked up instruments and found they could magically play right along with the sweet angelic music.

After a while the children became so relaxed, they decided to snuggle up for a nap on a bed of sound.

When they woke up, the music was still playing softly. So Alexander and Sophia tiptoed quietly out of the room, gently closing the door behind them.

The next door was pink with green spots and had a 4 on the outside. The eager children swung open the door, jumping with joy to see toys. So many toys! Firetrucks! Cars! Airplanes! Trains! Blocks! Dollhouses! Paints! Costumes! Stuffed animals! Every toy they'd ever dreamed of and some they'd never seen before! Alexander and Sophia raced into the room to play with everything they could get their gleeful hands on.

Alexander grabbed a fireman's hat, threw on a fireman's coat and drove around on a toy firetruck, then engineered a train and piloted a plane. "Look at this knight's sword!" Alexander beamed as he grasped the embroidered play sword. He picked up a shield, rode a horse and slayed a dragon. "Fear not, Sophia," Alexander bravely assured his sister. "Sir Alexander shall protect you!"

Sophia slipped into a pretty princess dress, donned a sparkling tiara and waved a magic wand, turning stuffed animals into cute little creatures that playfully jumped at her feet. She tied on a cape, flew around the room, had tea with her favorite dolls, and gave her brother a ride in a toy car. While driving, Sophia turned to Alexander and exclaimed, "Isn't this amazing?! Weeeeee!"

Playing with the toys was a blast, but Alexander and Sophia were curious about the rest of the rooms.

The kids hurried from the toy room and ran to door 5. The door was brown with no spots, no stripes, no other color. They opened it up expecting to find more fantastic fun, but the room was filled with plain brown furniture and boring household items.

Alexander and Sophia were momentarily disappointed, but quickly noticed a sugary-sweet smell. They put their noses closer to the bed. Sniff, sniff. It smelled like… They took a nibble… Yes, it was… CHOCOLATE!

Every single thing in the room was made of chocolate! Chocolate pillows, pencils, markers, crayons, beds, doorknobs, chairs and lamps! They bit into just about anything and everything in the entire room. Alexander found a small pencil to devour, and Sophia happily munched on an eraser. Yum, yum, yummy! Alexander and Sophia licked their chocolate-covered lips and fingers, then skipped and laughed their way to the sixth room.

The sixth room opened up to a big, bright green floor. They jumped on the floor and bounced all the way up to the ceiling, falling back down to bounce again and again. The whole room was bouncy! Walls, floor, ceiling! The children flipped, twirled, sprang and giggled until their tired legs felt like noodles and could bounce no more.

Alexander and Sophia slowly let themselves bounce to the ground and carefully crawled to the door without springing up again.

Still one more room to go. It was getting late, and they had a long journey home. Alexander and Sophia walked up to the final door. It was a gleaming gold color. They took a deep breath and pushed together on the 7th door. And what did they find?

To their surprise, it was their own bedroom. They were back home. It was indeed a magic house!

Their hearts still glowing from an unforgettably magnificent day, Alexander and Sophia rolled into their beds. They pulled the sheets snugly up to their cheeks and softly drifted into fun, adventure-filled dreams.

THE END

54328635R00021

Made in the USA
San Bernardino, CA
13 October 2017